Gertrude Chandler Warner's

THE BOXC
CHILD

THE LIGHTHOUSE MYSTERY

When the Alden children take a summer trip to the New England coast, they have a fun place to stay—a lighthouse! But strange things happen after it gets dark, and Watch wakes up growling at night. Can the Boxcar Children shed light on a seaside mystery?

THE BOXCAR CHILDREN
GRAPHIC NOVELS

THE BOXCAR CHILDREN
SURPRISE ISLAND
THE YELLOW HOUSE MYSTERY
MYSTERY RANCH
MIKE'S MYSTERY
BLUE BAY MYSTERY
SNOWBOUND MYSTERY
TREE HOUSE MYSTERY
THE HAUNTED CABIN MYSTERY
THE AMUSEMENT PARK MYSTERY
THE PIZZA MYSTERY
THE CASTLE MYSTERY
THE WOODSHED MYSTERY
THE LIGHTHOUSE MYSTERY
MOUNTAIN TOP MYSTERY

Gertrude Chandler Warner's

THE BOXCAR CHILDREN
THE LIGHTHOUSE MYSTERY

Adapted by Joeming Dunn
Illustrated by Ben Dunn

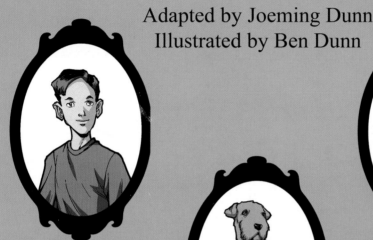

Henry Alden

Watch

Jessie Alden

Violet Alden

Benny Alden

Visit us at www.albertwhitman.com.

Adapted by Joeming Dunn
Illustrated by Ben Dunn
Colored by Robby Bevard
Lettered by Joeming Dunn & Doug Dlin
Edited by Stephanie Hedlund
Interior layout and design by Kristen Fitzner Denton
Cover art by Ben Dunn
Book design and packaging by Shannon Eric Denton

Library of Congress Cataloging-in-Publication Data
is available from the Library of Congress.

10 9 8 7 6 5 4 3 2 1 LB 15 14 13 12 11 10

Gertrude Chandler Warner's

THE BOXCAR CHILDREN GRAPHIC NOVELS

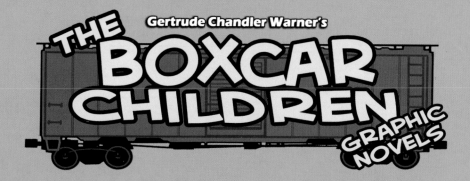

THE LIGHTHOUSE MYSTERY

Contents

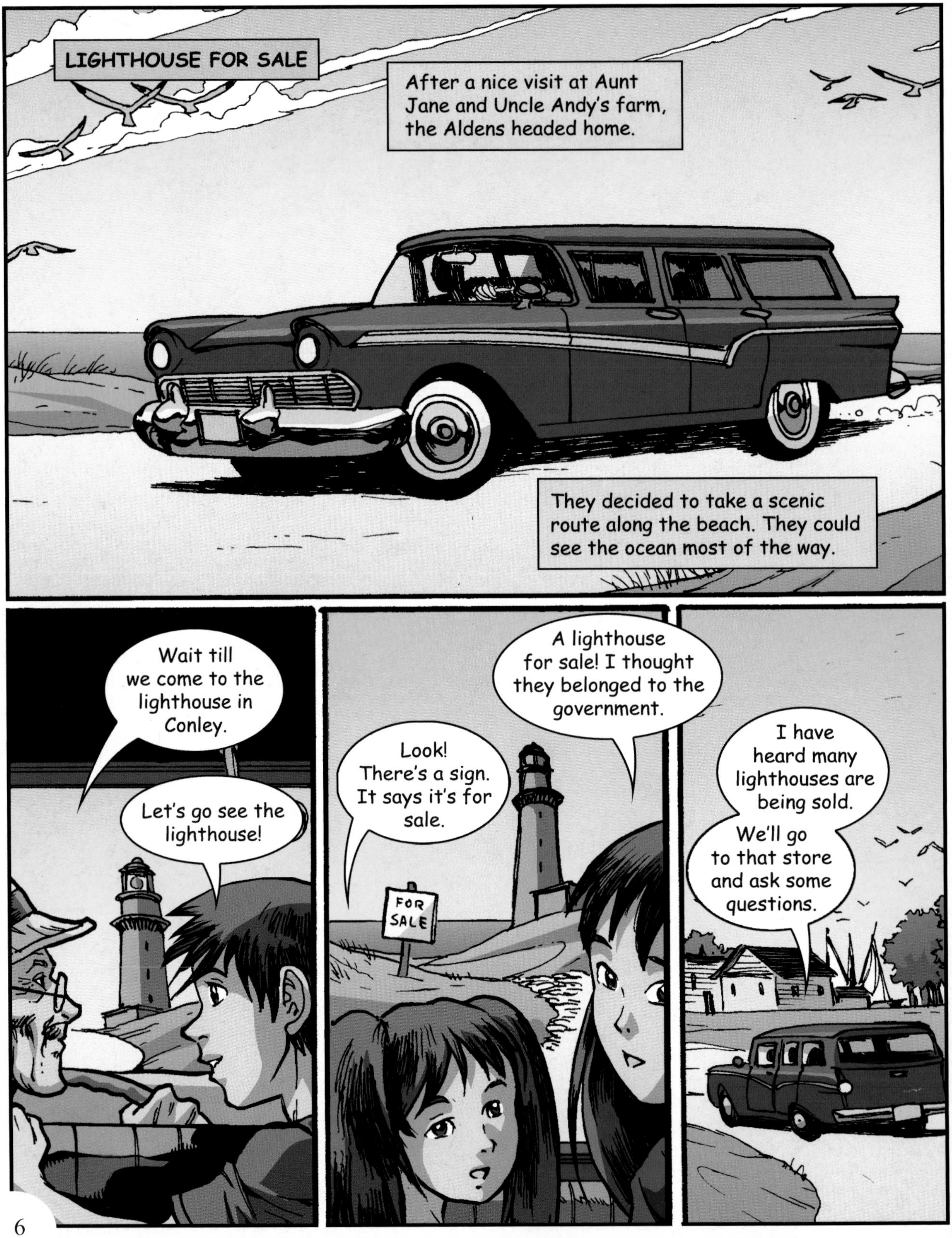
LIGHTHOUSE FOR SALE
After a nice visit at Aunt Jane and Uncle Andy's farm, the Aldens headed home.
They decided to take a scenic route along the beach. They could see the ocean most of the way.
Wait till we come to the lighthouse in Conley.
Let's go see the lighthouse!
A lighthouse for sale! I thought they belonged to the government.
Look! There's a sign. It says it's for sale.
FOR SALE
I have heard many lighthouses are being sold.
We'll go to that store and ask some questions.

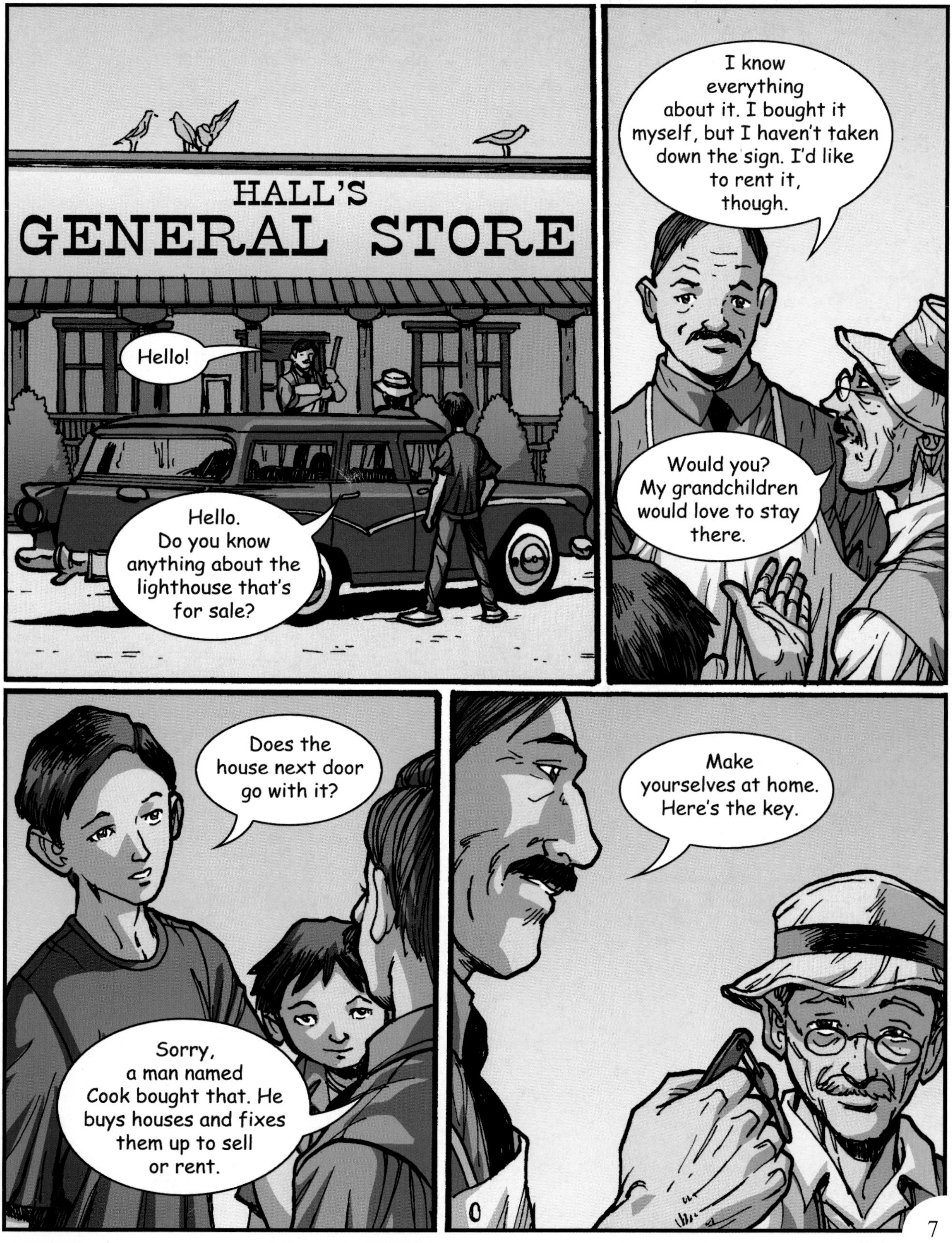
HALL'S
GENERAL STORE
Hello!
Hello.
Do you know anything about the lighthouse that's for sale?
I know everything about it. I bought it myself, but I haven't taken down the sign. I'd like to rent it, though.
Would you? My grandchildren would love to stay there.
Does the house next door go with it?
Sorry, a man named Cook bought that. He buys houses and fixes them up to sell or rent.
Make yourselves at home. Here's the key.

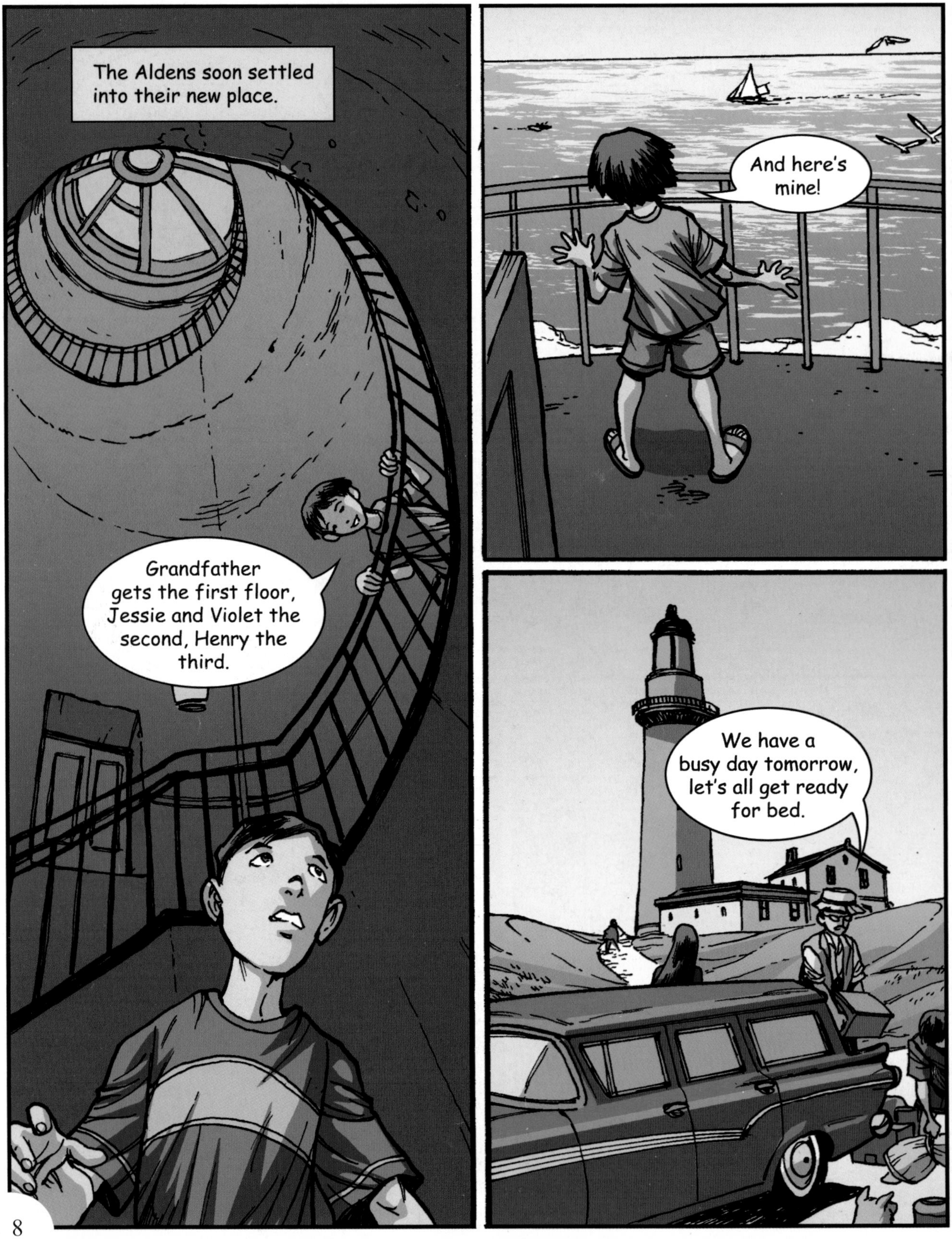
The Aldens soon settled into their new place.
Grandfather gets the first floor, Jessie and Violet the second, Henry the third.
And here's mine!
We have a busy day tomorrow, let's all get ready for bed.

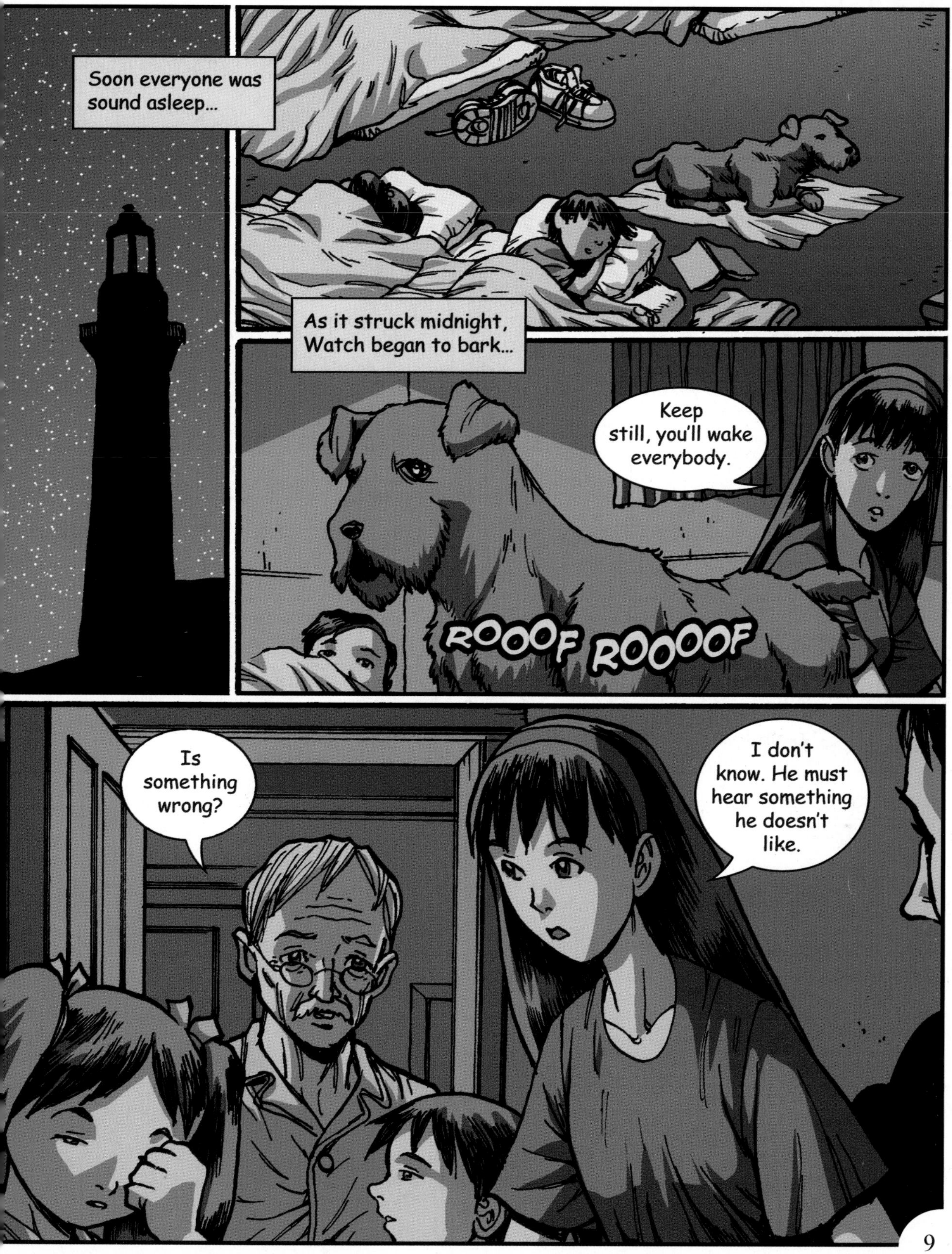

Soon everyone was sound asleep...
As it struck midnight, Watch began to bark...
Keep still, you'll wake everybody.
ROOOF ROOOOF
Is something wrong?
I don't know. He must hear something he doesn't like.

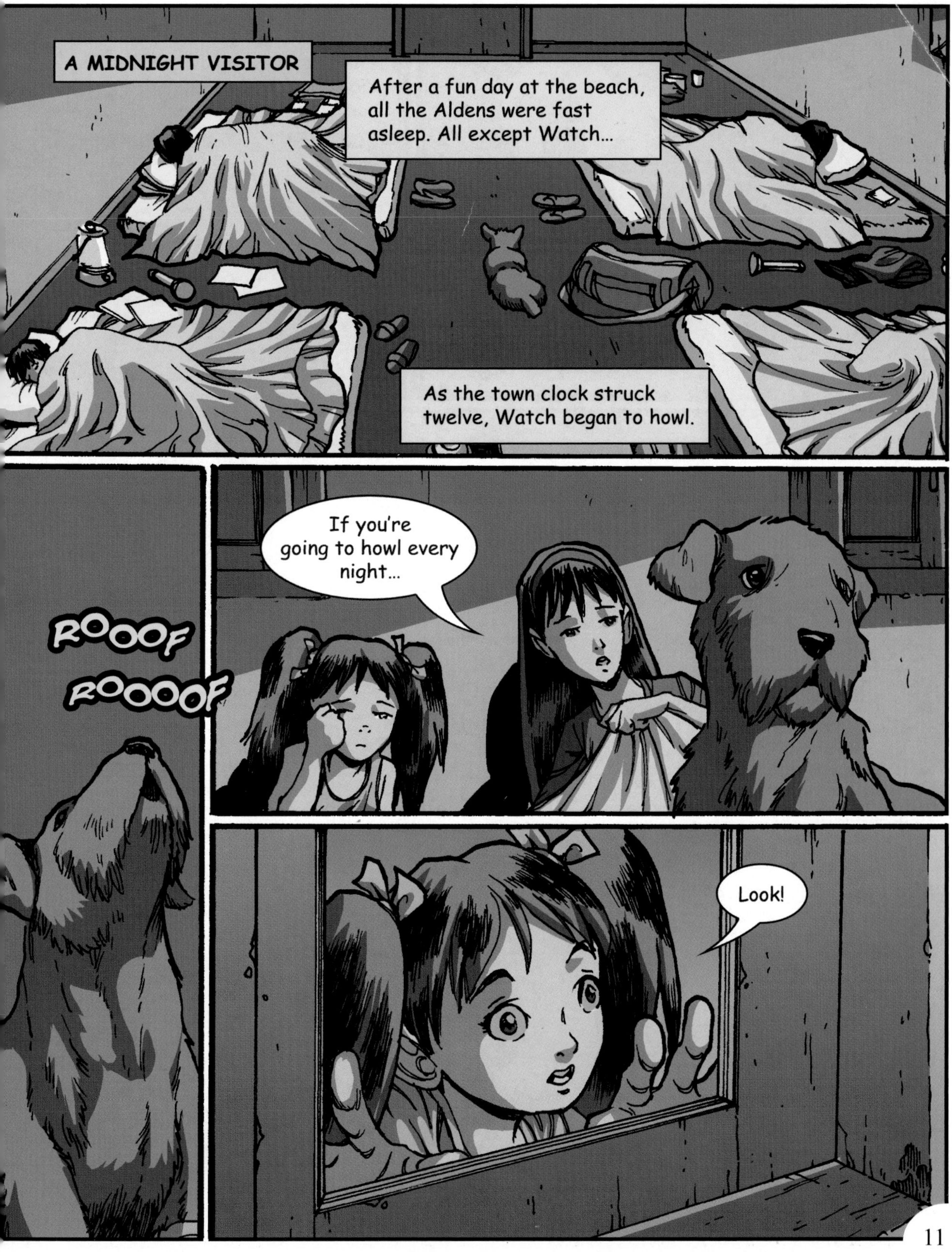

A MIDNIGHT VISITOR
After a fun day at the beach, all the Aldens were fast asleep. All except Watch...
As the town clock struck twelve, Watch began to howl.
ROOOF
ROOOOF
If you're going to howl every night...
Look!

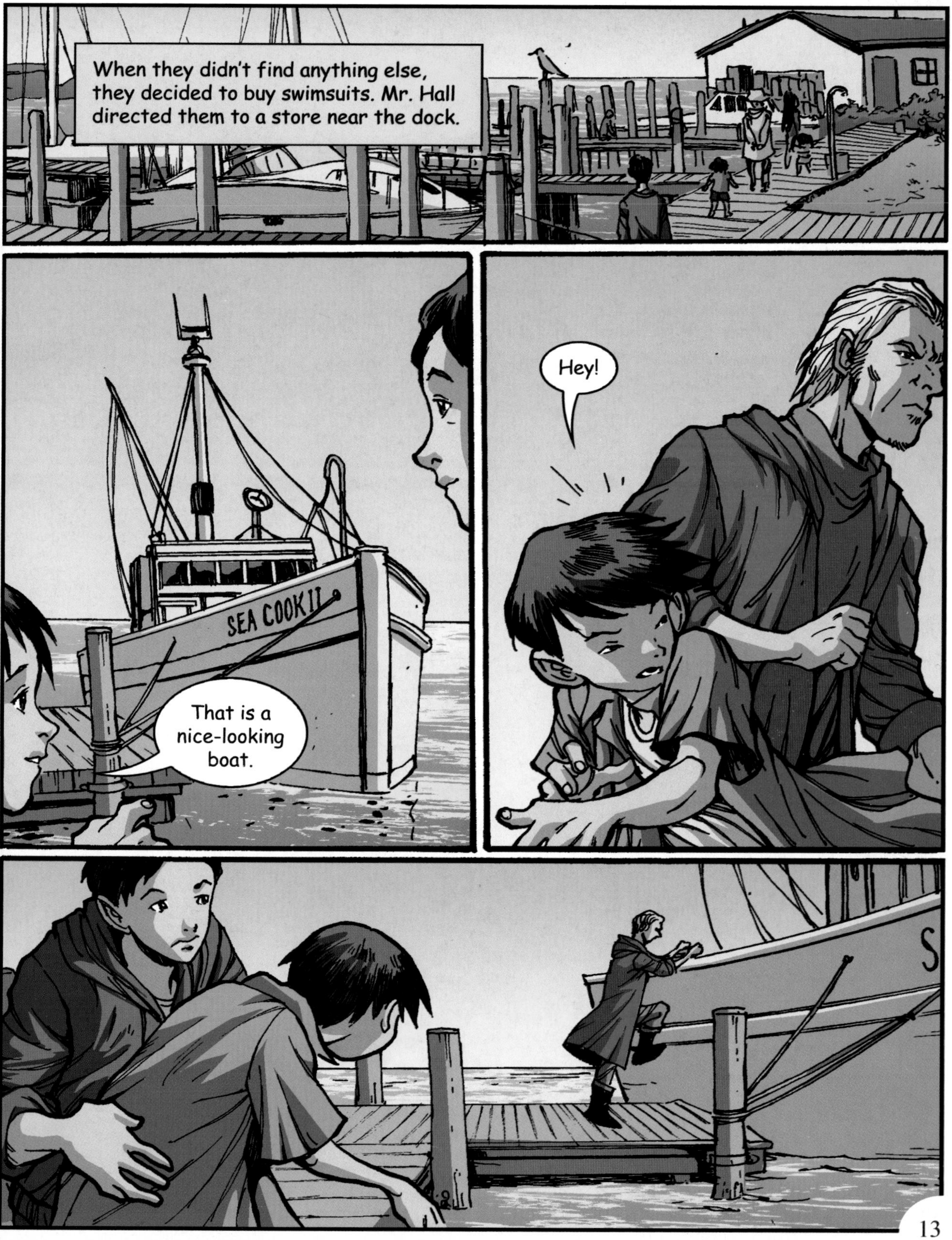
When they didn't find anything else, they decided to buy swimsuits. Mr. Hall directed them to a store near the dock.
SEA COOK II
That is a nice-looking boat.
Hey!

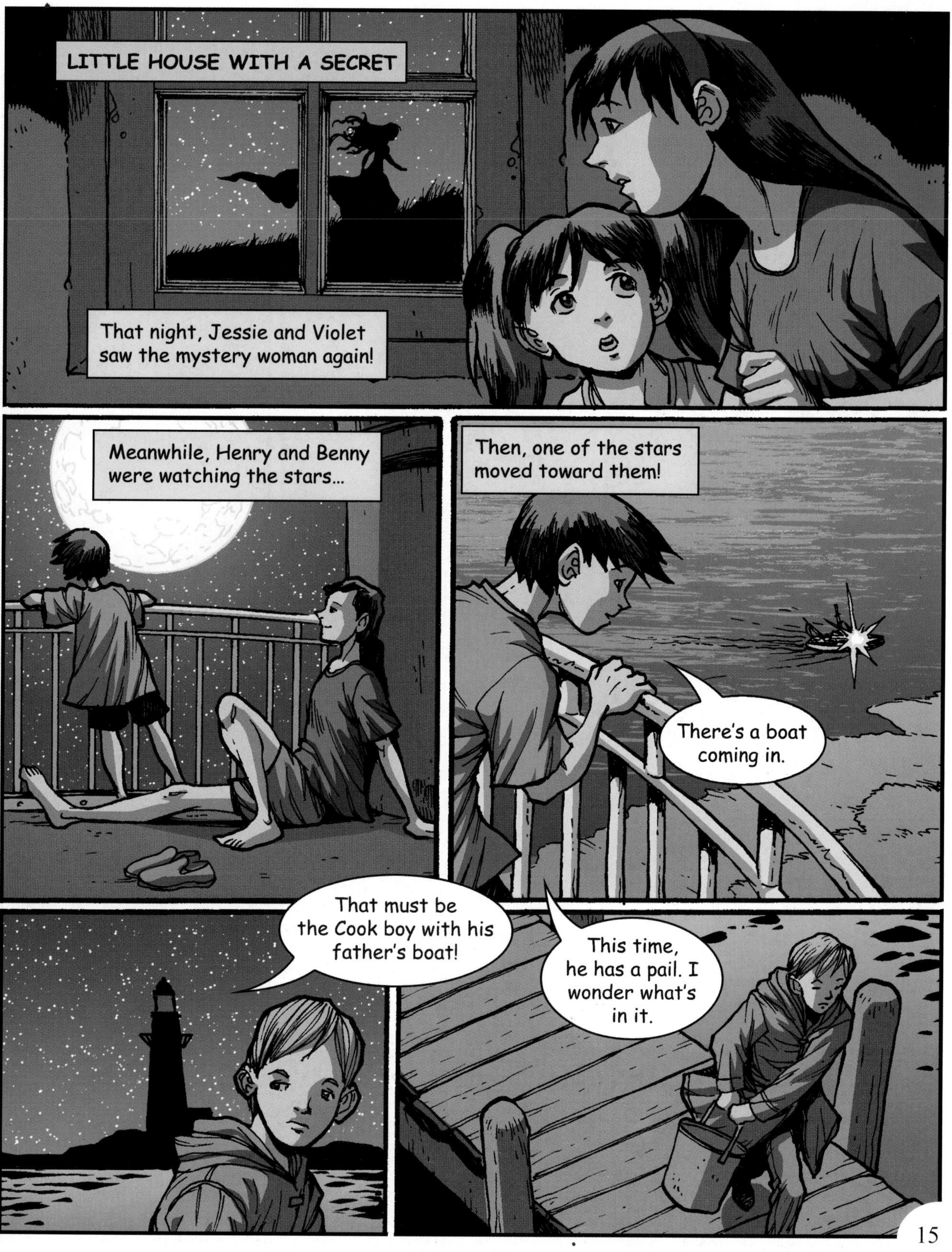
LITTLE HOUSE WITH A SECRET
That night, Jessie and Violet saw the mystery woman again!
Meanwhile, Henry and Benny were watching the stars...
Then, one of the stars moved toward them!
There's a boat coming in.
That must be the Cook boy with his father's boat!
This time, he has a pail. I wonder what's in it.

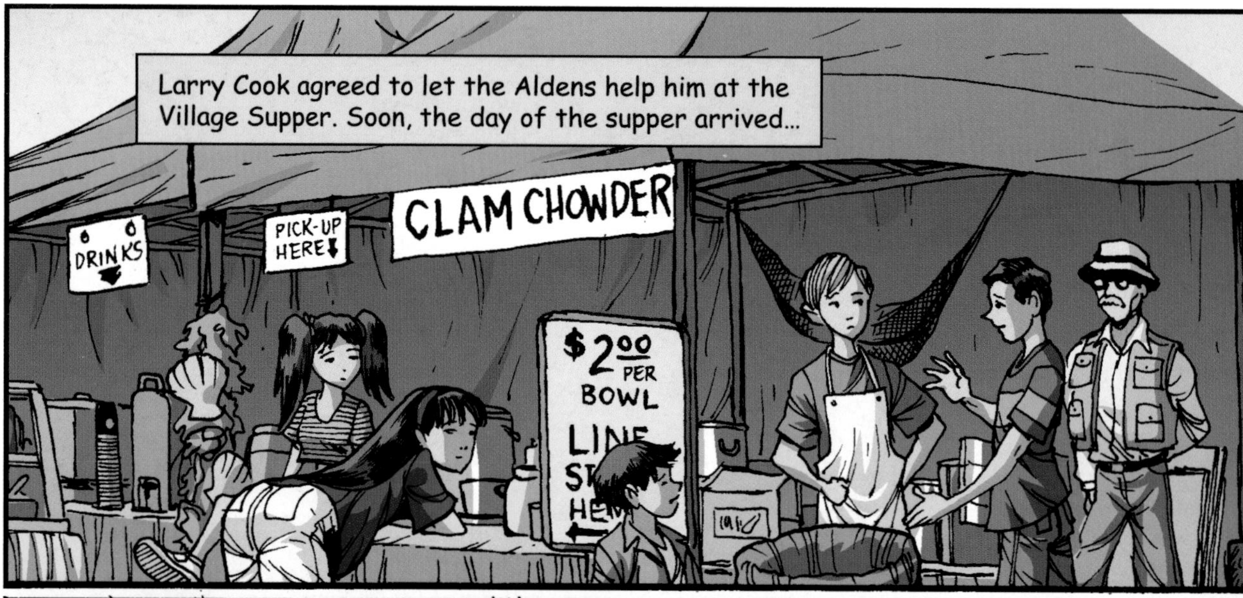
Larry Cook agreed to let the Aldens help him at the Village Supper. Soon, the day of the supper arrived...
DRINKS
PICK-UP HERE
CLAM CHOWDER
$2.00 PER BOWL

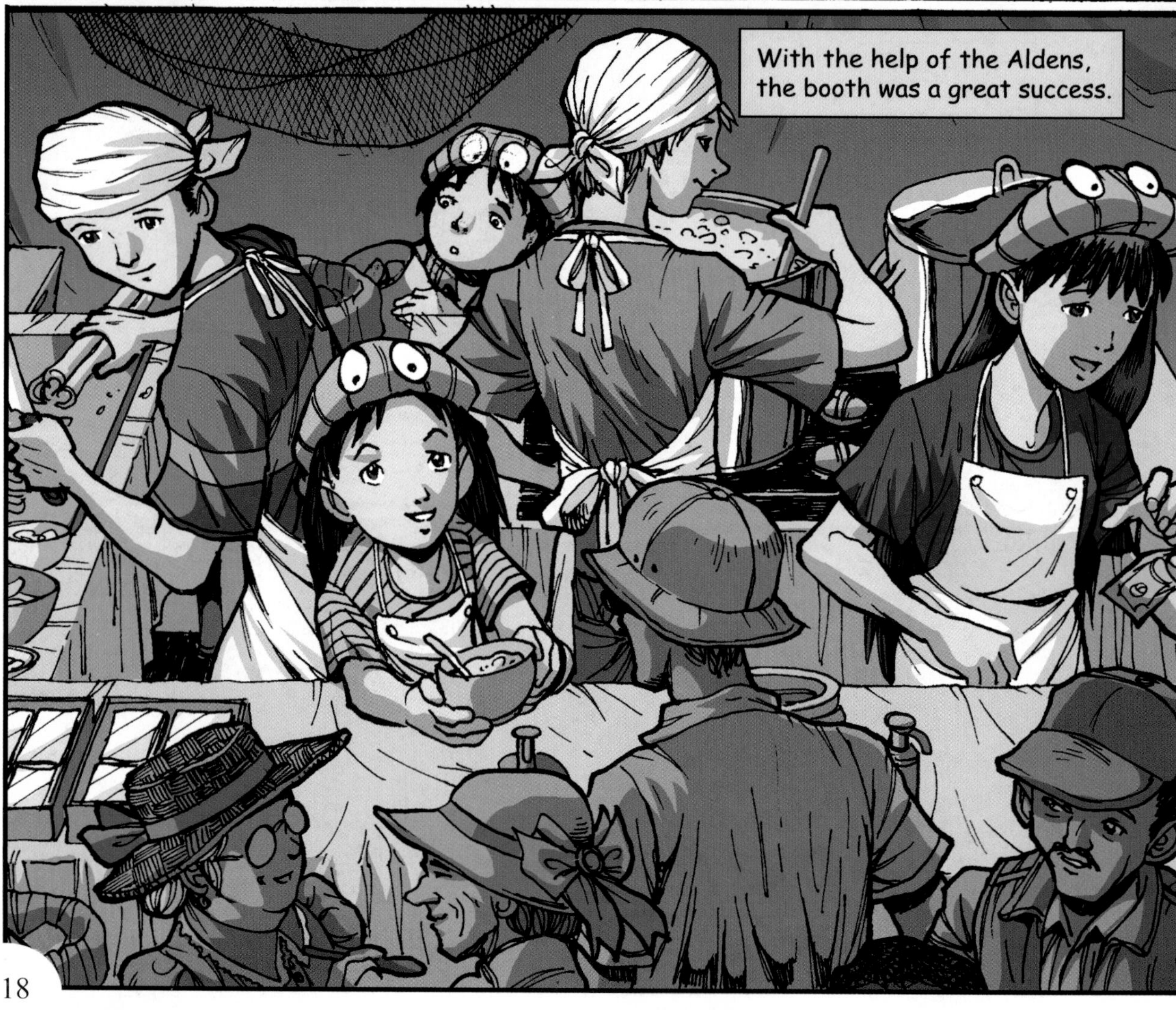
With the help of the Aldens, the booth was a great success.

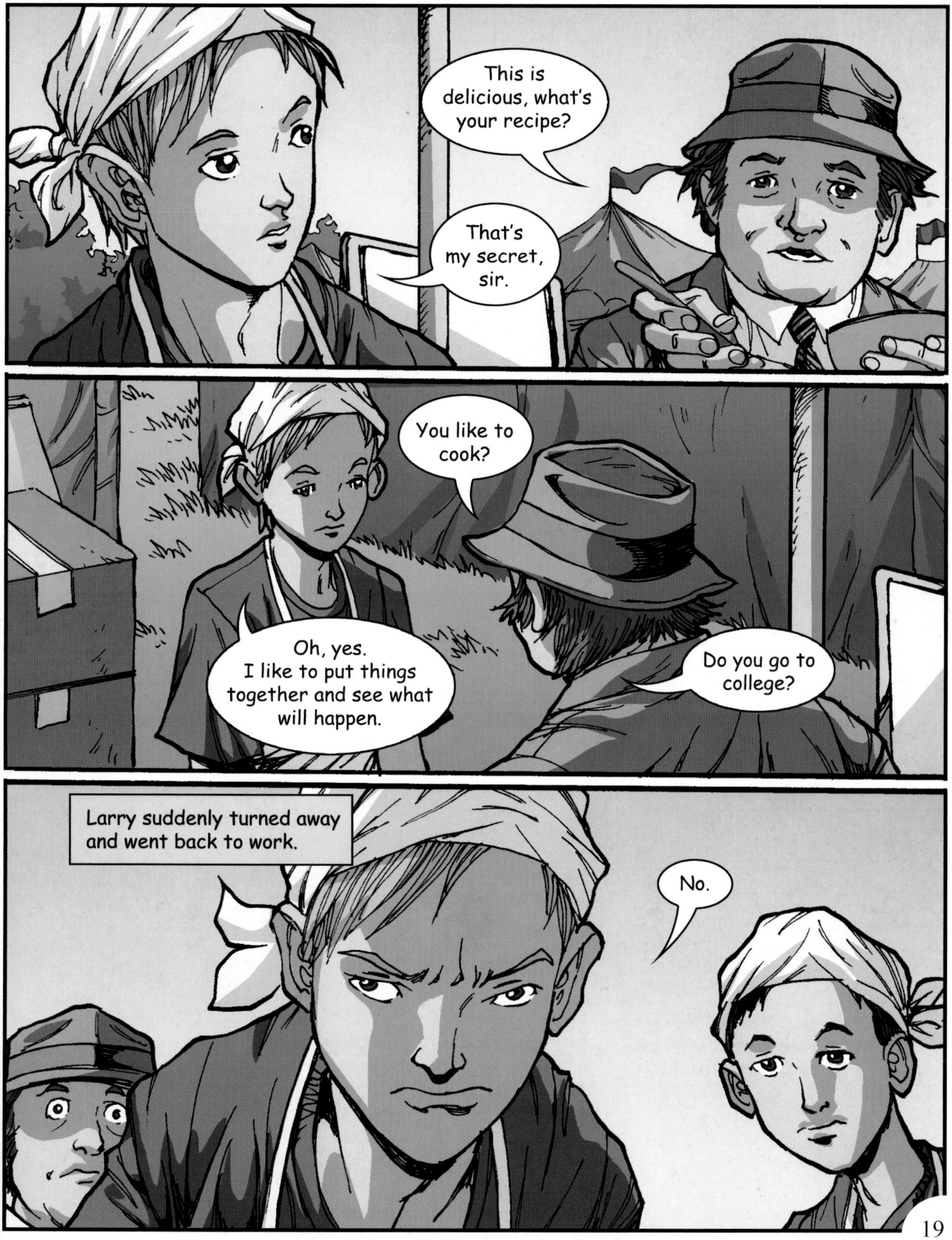
This is delicious, what's your recipe?
That's my secret, sir.
You like to cook?
Oh, yes. I like to put things together and see what will happen.
Do you go to college?
Larry suddenly turned away and went back to work.
No.

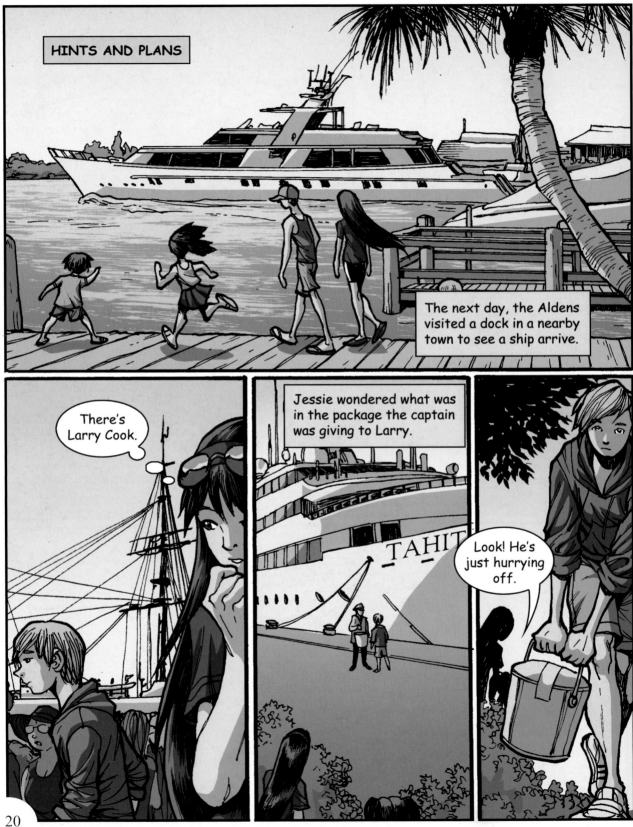

HINTS AND PLANS

The next day, the Aldens visited a dock in a nearby town to see a ship arrive.

There's Larry Cook.

Jessie wondered what was in the package the captain was giving to Larry.

TAHITI

Look! He's just hurrying off.

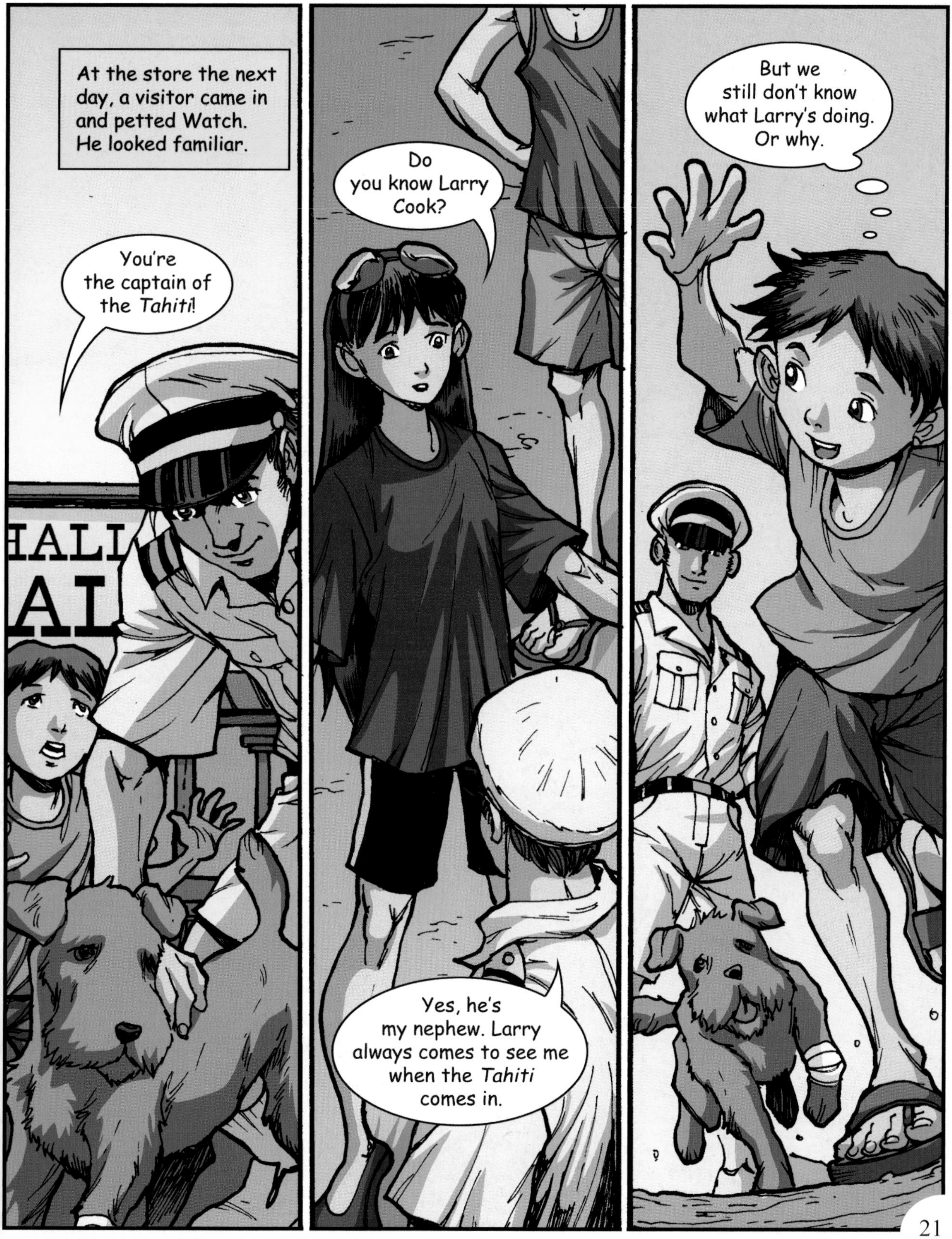
At the store the next day, a visitor came in and petted Watch. He looked familiar.
You're the captain of the *Tahiti*!
Do you know Larry Cook?
Yes, he's my nephew. Larry always comes to see me when the *Tahiti* comes in.
But we still don't know what Larry's doing. Or why.
HALI
AL

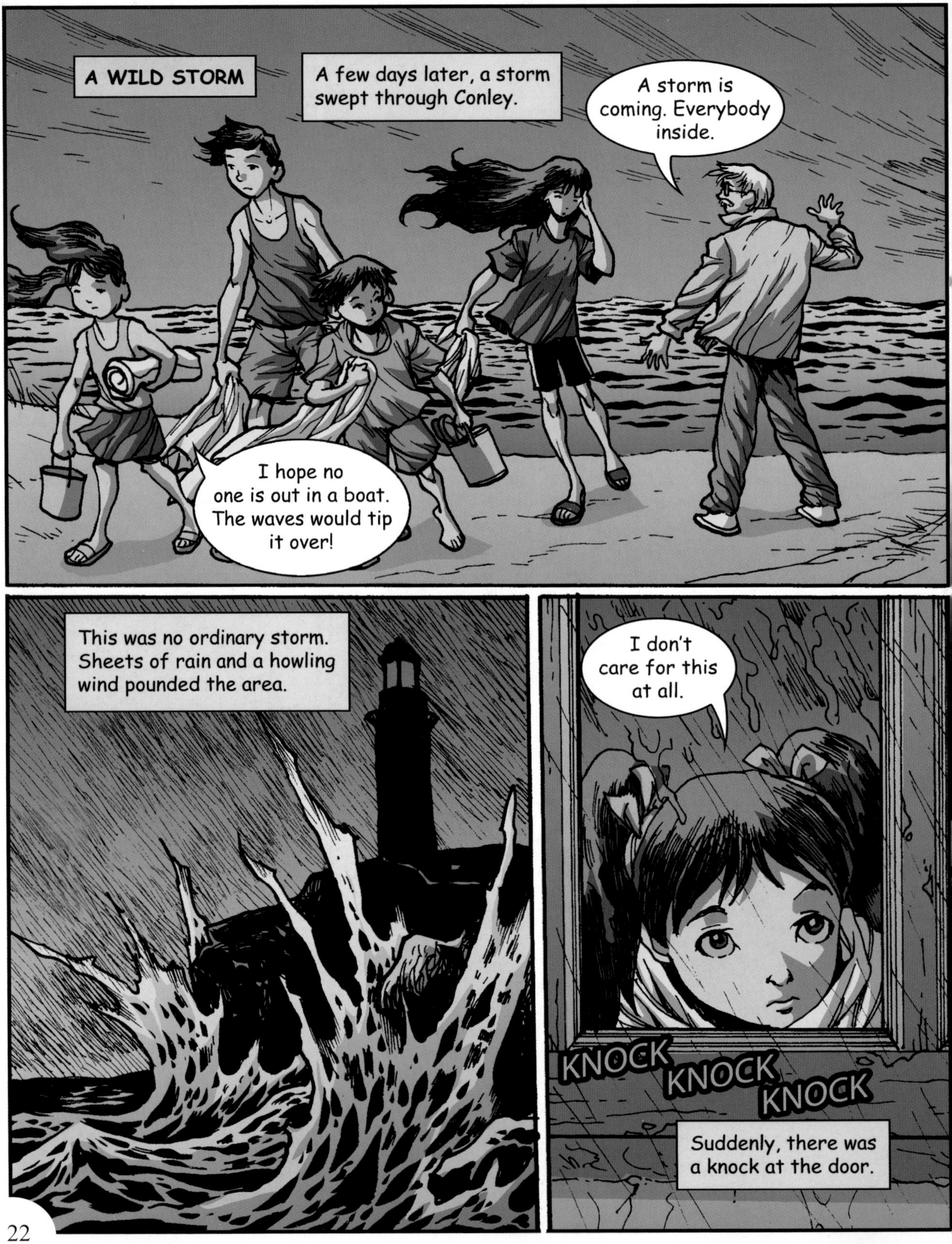
A WILD STORM
A few days later, a storm swept through Conley.
A storm is coming. Everybody inside.
I hope no one is out in a boat. The waves would tip it over!
This was no ordinary storm. Sheets of rain and a howling wind pounded the area.
I don't care for this at all.
KNOCK KNOCK KNOCK
Suddenly, there was a knock at the door.

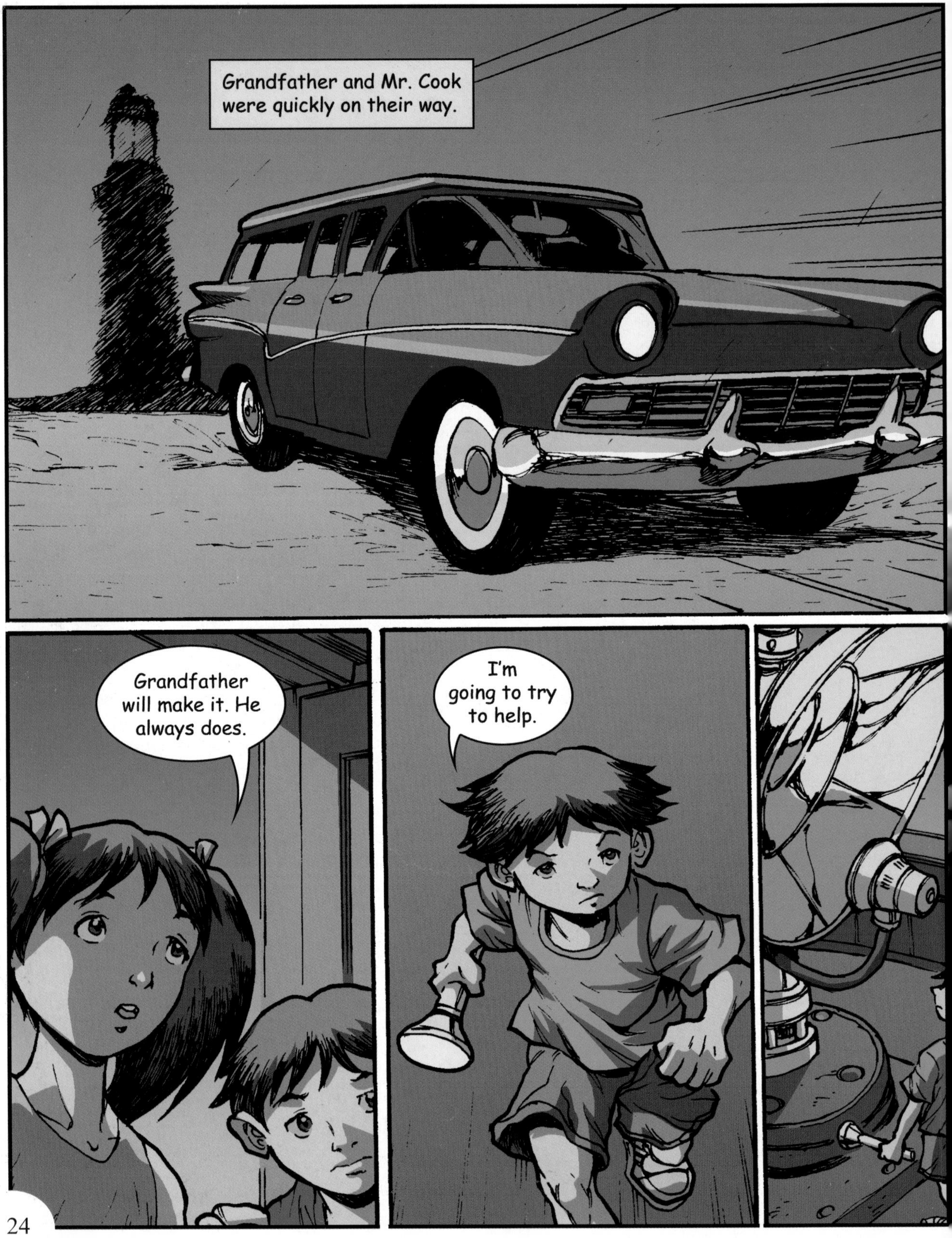
Grandfather and Mr. Cook were quickly on their way.
Grandfather will make it. He always does.
I'm going to try to help.

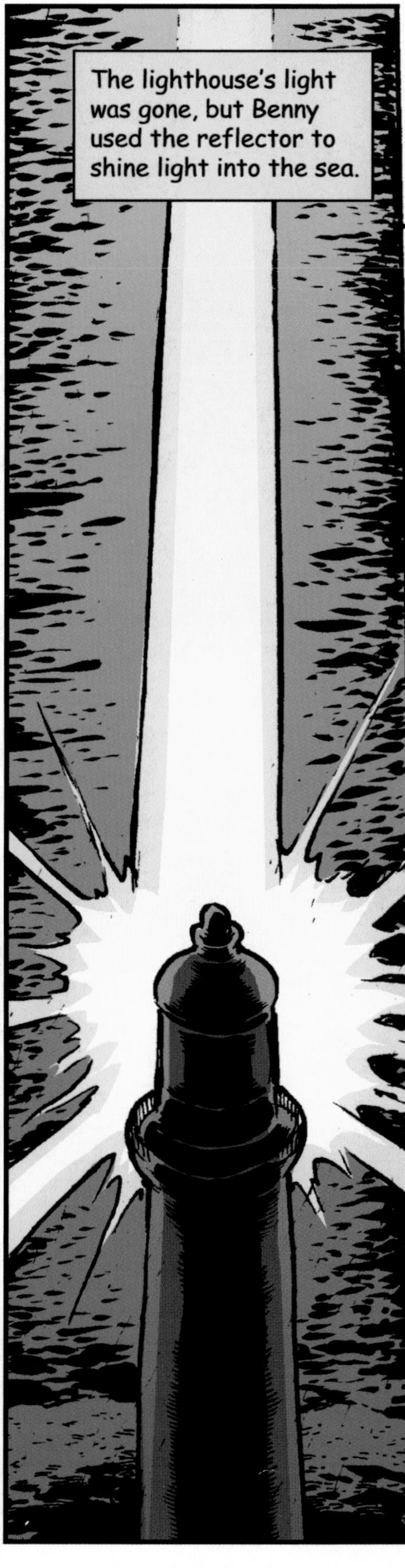
The lighthouse's light was gone, but Benny used the reflector to shine light into the sea.

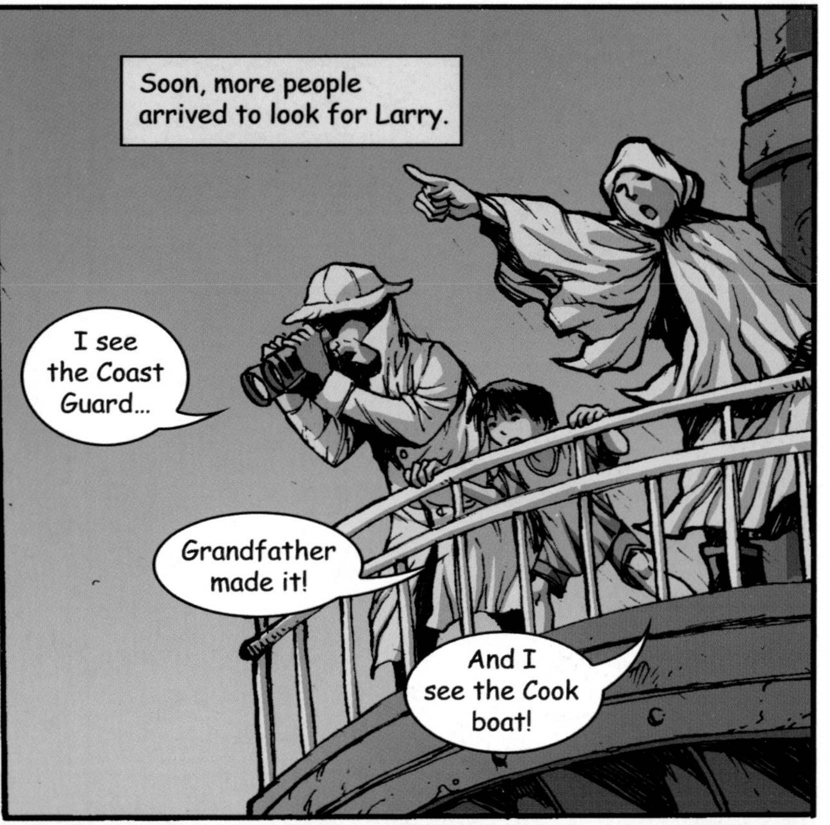
Soon, more people arrived to look for Larry.
I see the Coast Guard...
Grandfather made it!
And I see the Cook boat!

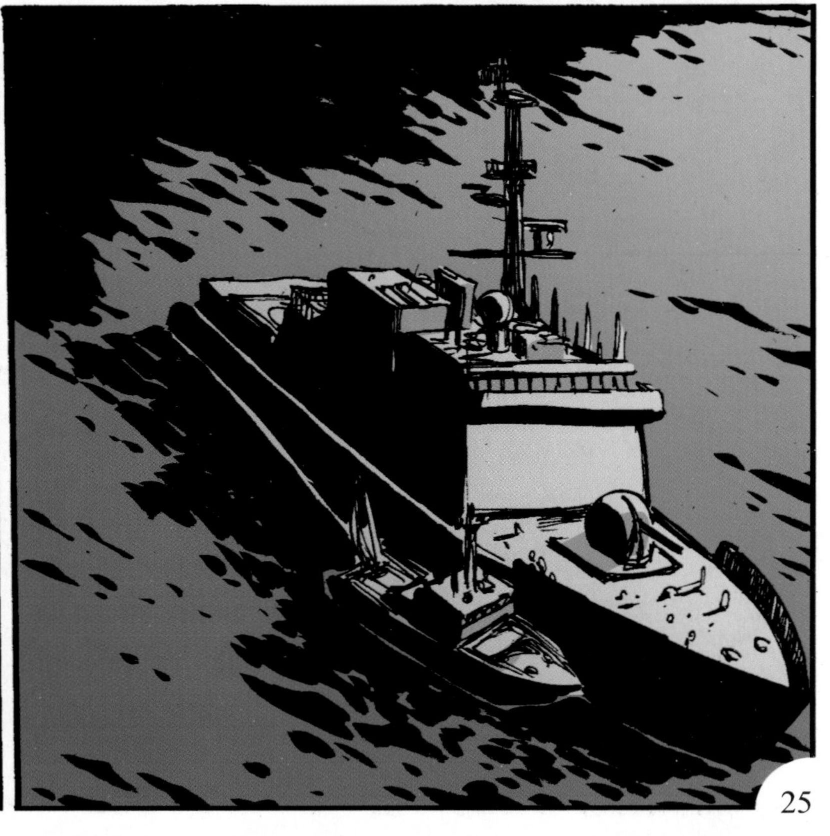

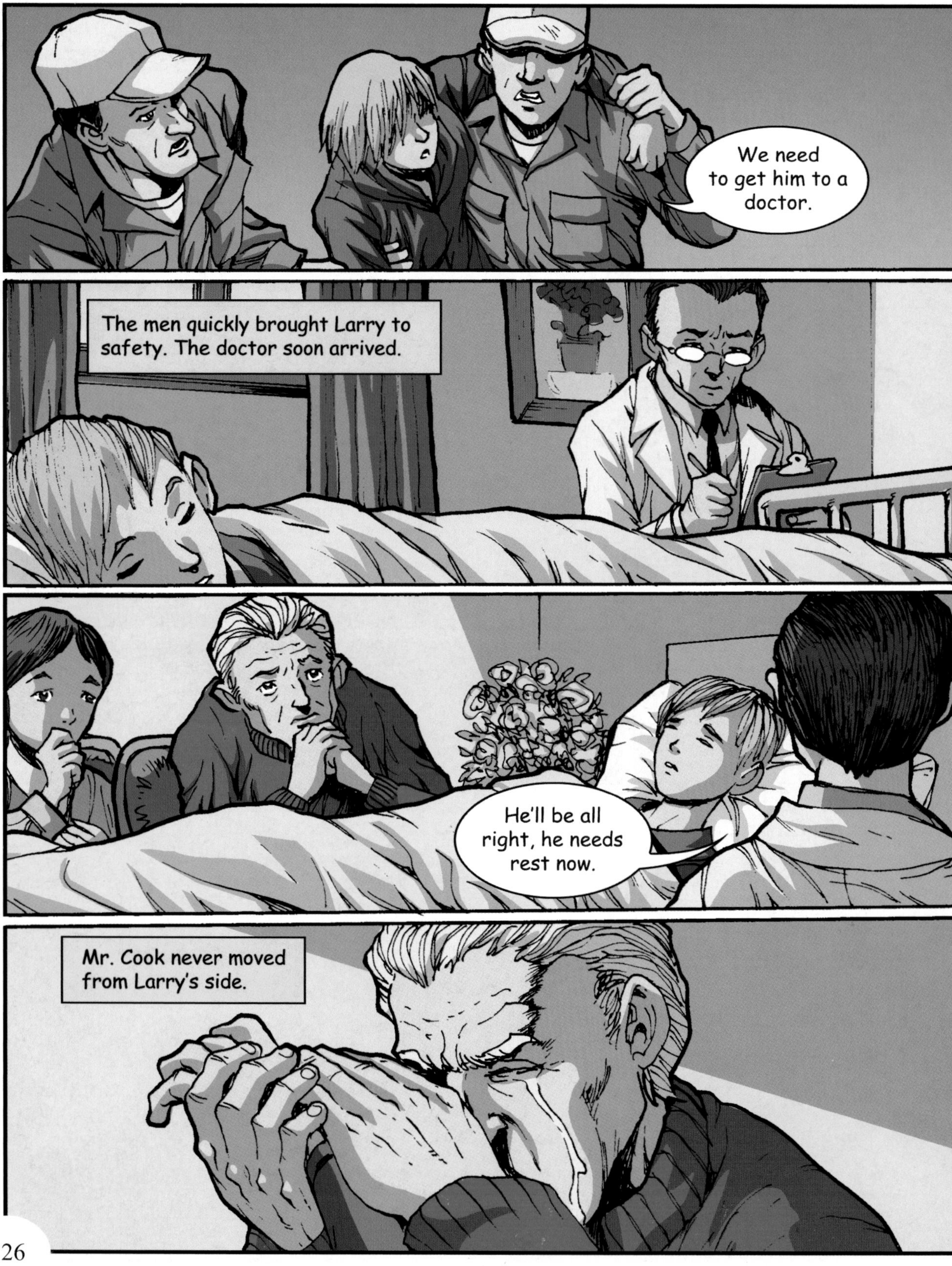
We need to get him to a doctor.
The men quickly brought Larry to safety. The doctor soon arrived.
He'll be all right, he needs rest now.
Mr. Cook never moved from Larry's side.

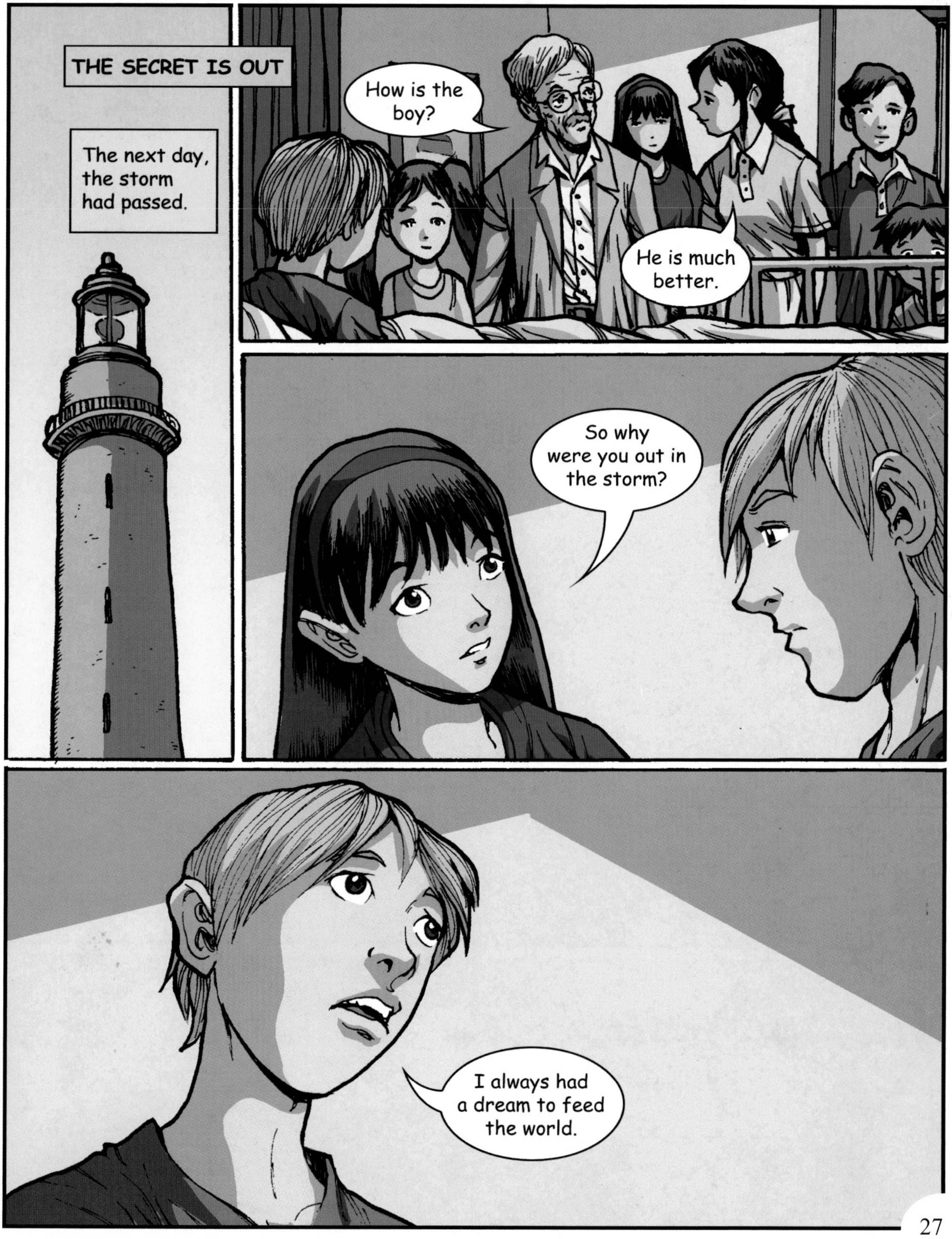
THE SECRET IS OUT
The next day, the storm had passed.
How is the boy?
He is much better.
So why were you out in the storm?
I always had a dream to feed the world.

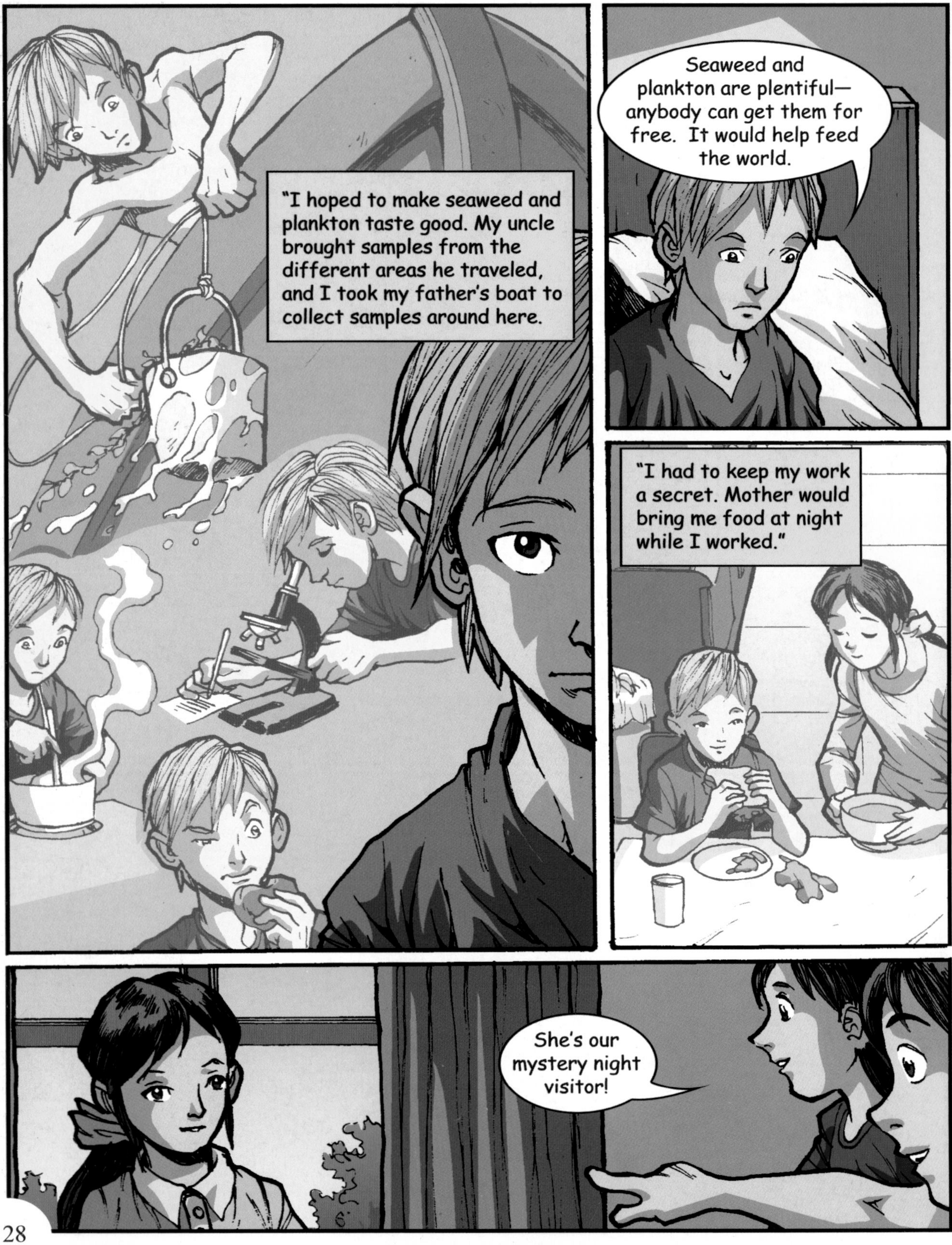
"I hoped to make seaweed and plankton taste good. My uncle brought samples from the different areas he traveled, and I took my father's boat to collect samples around here.
Seaweed and plankton are plentiful—anybody can get them for free. It would help feed the world.
"I had to keep my work a secret. Mother would bring me food at night while I worked."
She's our mystery night visitor!

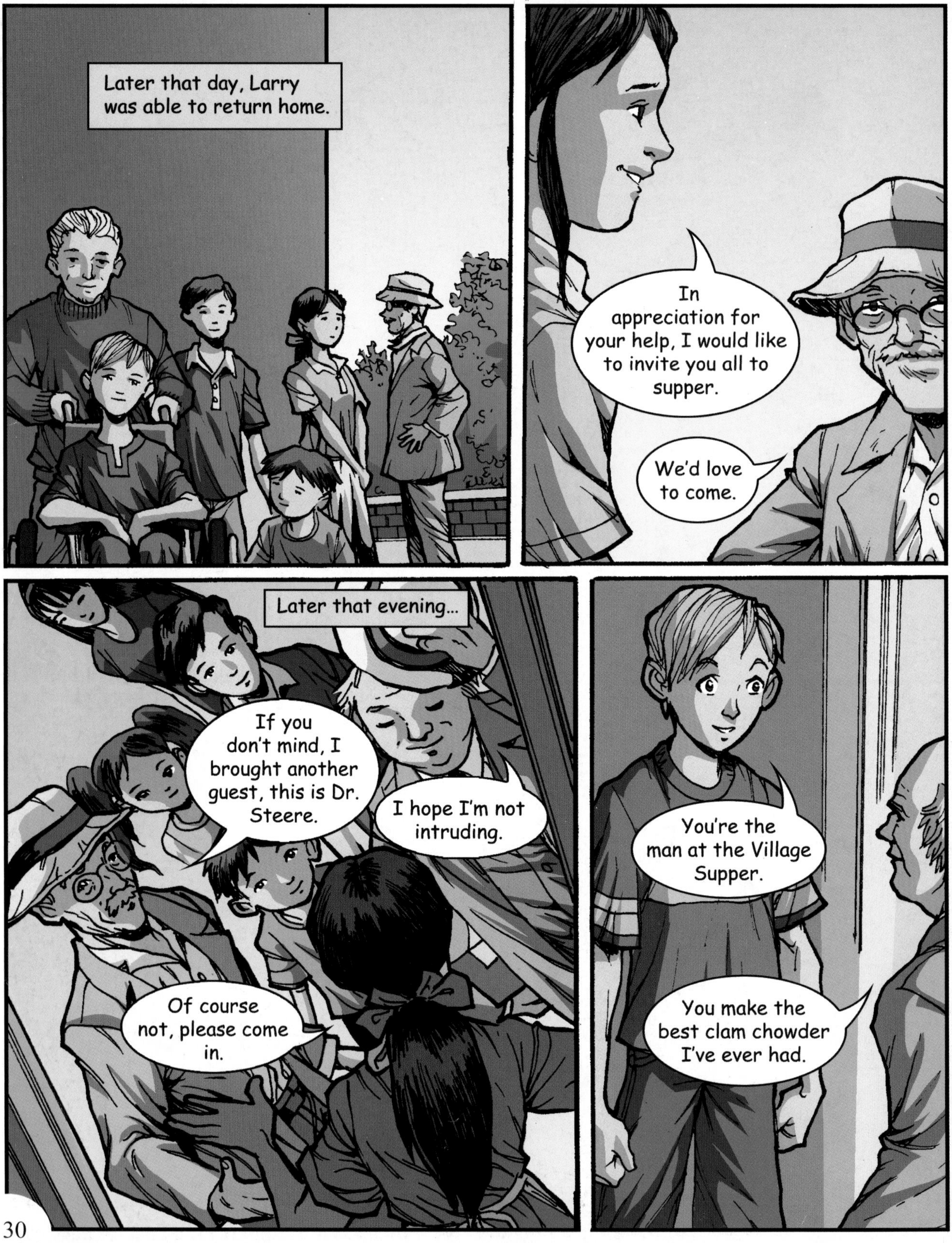
Later that day, Larry was able to return home.
In appreciation for your help, I would like to invite you all to supper.
We'd love to come.
Later that evening...
If you don't mind, I brought another guest, this is Dr. Steere.
I hope I'm not intruding.
Of course not, please come in.
You're the man at the Village Supper.
You make the best clam chowder I've ever had.

ABOUT THE CREATOR

Gertrude Chandler Warner was born on April 16, 1890, in Putnam, Connecticut. In 1918, Warner began teaching at Israel Putnam School. As a teacher, she discovered that many readers who liked an exciting story could not find books that were both easy and fun to read. She decided to try to meet this need. In 1942, *The Boxcar Children* was published for these readers.

Warner drew on her own experience to write *The Boxcar Children*. As a child she spent hours watching trains go by on the tracks near her family home. She often dreamed about what it would be like to live in a caboose or freight car—just as the Alden children do.

When readers asked for more Alden adventures, Warner began additional stories. While the mystery element is central to each of the books, she never thought of them as strictly juvenile mysteries. She liked to stress the Aldens' independence. Henry, Jessie, Violet, and Benny go about most of their adventures with as little adult supervision as possible—something that delights young readers.

During her lifetime, Warner received hundreds of letters from fans as she continued the Aldens' adventures, writing nineteen Boxcar Children books in all. After her death in 1979, her publisher, Albert Whitman and Company, carried on Warner's vision. Today, the Boxcar Children series has more than 100 books.